How Santa Lost His Job

By **Stephen Krensky**

Illustrated by **S. D. Schindler**

Aladdin Paperbacks

New York London Toronto Sydney

First Aladdin Paperbacks edition October 2004

Text copyright © 2001 by Stephen Krensky
Illustrations copyright © 2001 by S. D. Schindler

ALADDIN PAPERBACKS
An imprint of Simon & Schuster
Children's Publishing Division
1230 Avenue of the Americas
New York, NY 10020

Also available in a Simon & Schuster Books for Young Readers hardcover edition.
Designed by Paul Zakris
The text of this book was set in 16-point Daily News Medium.

Manufactured in China
2 4 6 8 10 9 7 5 3 1

The Library of Congress has cataloged the hardcover edition as follows:
Krensky, Stephen.
How Santa lost his job / by Stephen Krensky ; illustrated by S. D. Schindler.—1st ed.
p. cm.
Summary: Frustrated by Santa's slowness at Christmastime, Muckle the elf creates a mechanical replacement
called the Deliverator and proposes a series of contests to prove that it can do Santa's job better than he can.
ISBN 0-689-83173-0 (hc.)
[1. Elves—Fiction. 2. Santa Claus—Fiction. 3. Christmas—Fiction.] I. Schindler, S. D., ill. II. Title.
PZ7.K883 Ho 2001
[E]—dc21
00-063537
ISBN 0-689-87147-3 (pbk.)

For Stephanie Owens Lurie
—S. K.

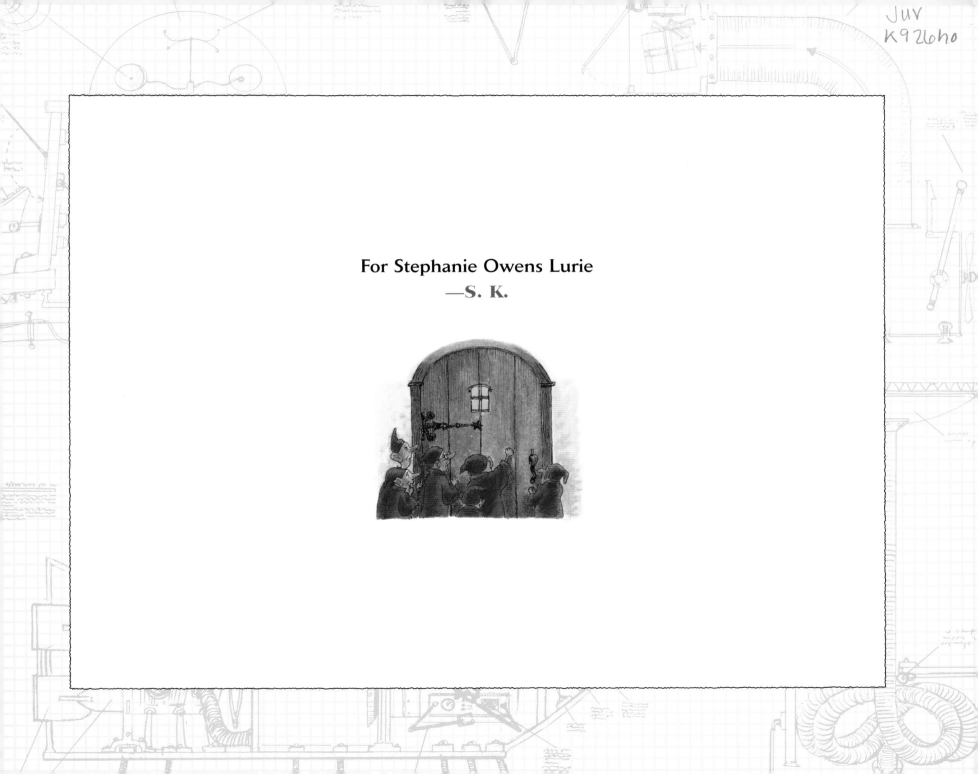

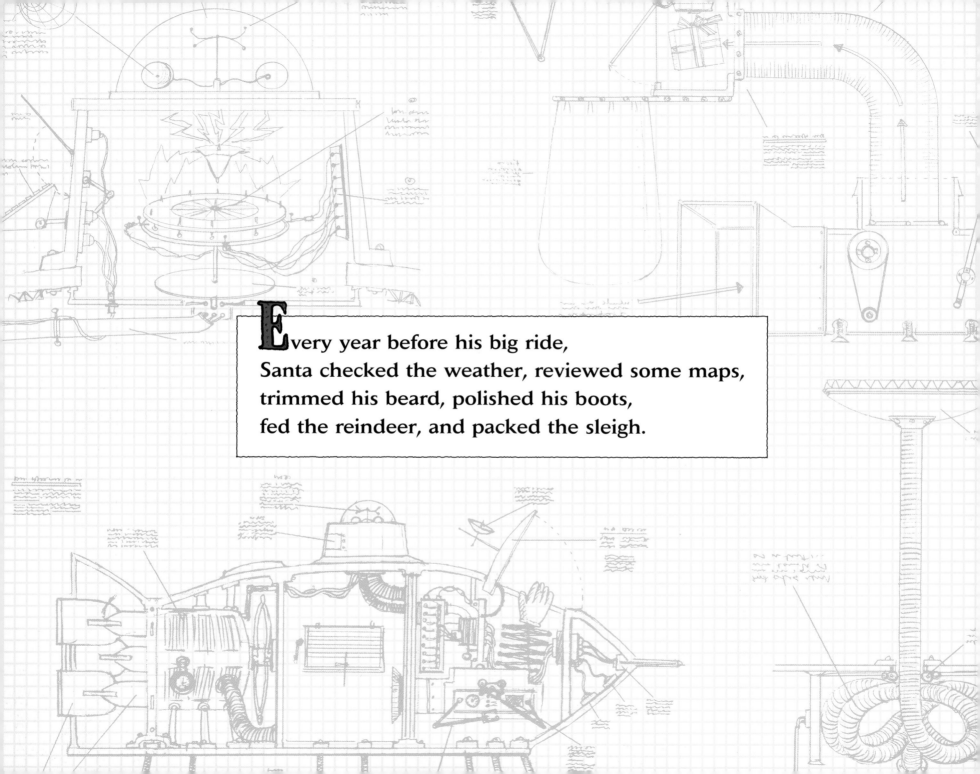

Every year before his big ride,
Santa checked the weather, reviewed some maps,
trimmed his beard, polished his boots,
fed the reindeer, and packed the sleigh.

He moved as fast as he could.
But even so, there was always a last-minute rush.

Some of the elves grumbled about this.
"Why can't Santa plan better?"
"How come he's so slow?"

One year an elf named Muckle said even more.

"Santa is too set in his ways," he declared.

"He wastes time and energy."

Maybe so, his friends agreed. But what could they do?

After all, Santa was only human.

That gave Muckle an idea.

For months he worked on a secret project,
and almost every day,
the mail carrier, Clara, dropped off packages at his door.
"What are you up to?" she asked.
But Muckle wouldn't say.
He kept his workshop locked and didn't let anyone in.

It was late fall when Muckle finally showed off his creation.
"This is the *Deliverator*!" he proclaimed.
The other elves admired the shiny metal and blinking lights.
"What does it do?" they asked.
"It's a replacement," said Muckle. "For Santa."

Muckle claimed the *Deliverator*
could travel around the world in one night.
It could go up and down chimneys with ease.
And it could deliver toys in the blink of an eye.

Clara heard the news as she made her rounds.
"But Santa already does those things," she told Muckle.
"Maybe so," he said,
"but the *Deliverator* will do them sooner, faster, and better."

The other elves were impressed.
However, they still needed proof.
"Fine," said Muckle. "Let's test Santa against the *Deliverator*.
The winner will deliver our toys from now on."

When Santa heard the news he shook his head.
"There's more to my job than meets the eye," he said.
"But since you make the toys, the decision is yours."

In the first contest, the elves timed how long it
took Santa and the *Deliverator* to get ready to leave.
Santa always started off with a bubble bath.
Then he carefully got dressed.
One of his boots usually gave him a little trouble.

The *Deliverator* didn't take baths or wear boots.
So it was ready first.

Next, Clara brought in two big stacks of mail.
She put one in front of Santa
and the other in front of the *Deliverator*.
A pile of toys sat between them.
"You have one hour," Muckle explained to Santa.
"Whoever matches the most children with a gift wins."

The *Deliverator* whirred and hummed,
scanning each request with lightning speed
and pairing it with a toy.

Santa read more slowly.
"Oh, I don't think he'd really like this," he murmured.
"And she didn't play with the one she got last year."
Before long he was hopelessly behind.

The third contest started out on two adjoining rooftops.

"Go!" shouted Muckle.

Santa and the *Deliverator* each raced down a chimney.

They both reached the bottom in a second
and put the toys under the tree.

But only Santa noticed the milk and cookies.
"Chocolate chip," he said. "My favorite."

The *Deliverator* didn't care about cookies.
It shot back out the chimney
while Santa was still drinking his milk.
"I told you!" Muckle shouted. "Santa is history."

The elves congratulated Muckle on his victory.
Only Clara still thought they were making a mistake.
"Santa isn't just about meeting a schedule," she said.
"He cares about getting things right."
But nobody would listen.
"We're sorry," the elves told Santa. "But business is business."

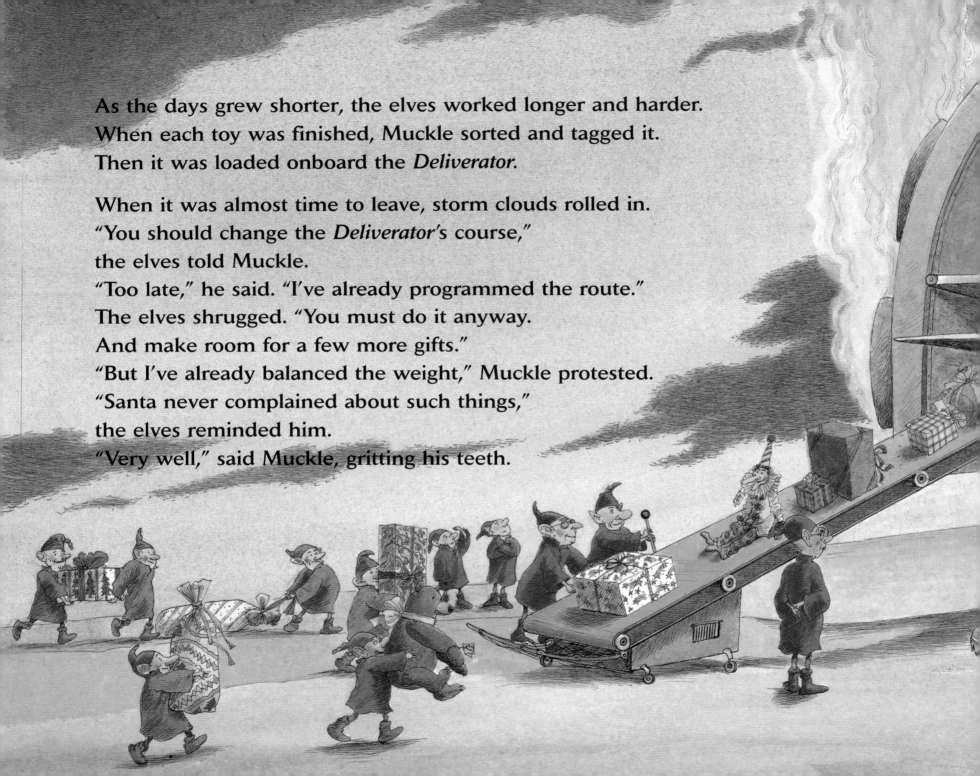

As the days grew shorter, the elves worked longer and harder.
When each toy was finished, Muckle sorted and tagged it.
Then it was loaded onboard the *Deliverator*.

When it was almost time to leave, storm clouds rolled in.
"You should change the *Deliverator*'s course,"
the elves told Muckle.
"Too late," he said. "I've already programmed the route."
The elves shrugged. "You must do it anyway.
And make room for a few more gifts."
"But I've already balanced the weight," Muckle protested.
"Santa never complained about such things,"
the elves reminded him.
"Very well," said Muckle, gritting his teeth.

He fiddled quickly with the dials and switches.
Then, fearing that the elves might ask for even more,
Muckle made a decision.
"Let's go!" he said, pressing a button.

The *Deliverator*'s rockets fired up and it took off
into the darkening sky.
But with all the extra weight and new directions,
the *Deliverator* seemed confused.
Instead of disappearing from sight, it kept circling overhead.
"Just a little more power," Muckle insisted.
He pressed one button after another.

The rockets glowed brighter.
The *Deliverator* spiraled around faster and faster.

When Santa arrived, the situation was all too clear.
The elves looked very uncomfortable.
"Santa, will you take your job back?" they asked. "Please?"
"Of course," Santa said, and left it at that.

Everyone, even Muckle, helped load the sleigh
and hitch up the reindeer.
It was their most hectic year yet.

After that, nobody talked of replacing Santa again.
Each year there were new delays or mix-ups.
But the elves didn't mind.
They realized now that this was all perfectly normal.

Still, not everything stayed the same.
Santa had learned a lot from the whole experience.
And as happy as he had been before,

he was even happier in the years to come.